ALSO BY LOUISE GLÜCK

The Wild Iris

BY

Louise Glück

An Imprint of HarperCollins Publishers

Acknowledgment is made to the editors of the following publications in which some of these poems first appeared:

American Poetry Review, The New York Times, The New Yorker ("Vespers: In Your Extended Absence," "Field Flowers," "The Silver Lily," and "The Gold Lily,") *Tikkun, Threepenny Review,* and *Yale Review.*

HarperCollins books may be purchased for educational, business, or sales promotional use. For information, please e-mail the Special Markets Department at SPsales@harpercollins.com.

Designed by Richard Oriolo

Library of Congress Cataloging-in-Publication Data

Glück, Louise.
    The wild iris / by Louise Glück.—1st ed.
        p.   cm.
    I. Title.
PS3557.L8W5   1992
811'54—dc20   91-36419   CIP
ISBN: 0-88001-281-1
ISBN: 0-88001-334-6 (paperback)

24 25 26 27 28 LBC 38 37 36 35 34

The Wild Iris

CONTENTS

FOR
Kathryn Davis
Meredith Hoppin
David Langston

FOR
John and Noah

The Wild Iris

THE WILD IRIS

At the end of my suffering
there was a door.

Hear me out: that which you call death
I remember.

Overhead, noises, branches of the pine shifting.
Then nothing. The weak sun
flickered over the dry surface.

It is terrible to survive
as consciousness
buried in the dark earth.

Then it was over: that which you fear, being
a soul and unable
to speak, ending abruptly, the stiff earth
bending a little. And what I took to be
birds darting in low shrubs.

You who do not remember
passage from the other world
I tell you I could speak again: whatever
returns from oblivion returns
to find a voice:

from the center of my life came
a great fountain, deep blue
shadows on azure seawater.

I

The sun shines; by the mailbox, leaves
of the divided birch tree folded, pleated like fins.
Underneath, hollow stems of the white daffodils,
    Ice Wings, Cantatrice; dark
leaves of the wild violet. Noah says
depressives hate the spring, imbalance
between the inner and the outer world. I make
another case—being depressed, yes, but in a sense passionately
attached to the living tree, my body
actually curled in the split trunk, almost at peace,
    in the evening rain
almost able to feel
sap frothing and rising: Noah says this is
an error of depressives, identifying
with a tree, whereas the happy heart
wanders the garden like a falling leaf, a figure for
the part, not the whole.

MATINS

Unreachable father, when we were first
exiled from heaven, you made
a replica, a place in one sense
different from heaven, being
designed to teach a lesson: otherwise
the same—beauty on either side, beauty
without alternative— Except
we didn't know what was the lesson. Left alone,
we exhausted each other. Years
of darkness followed; we took turns
working the garden, the first tears
filling our eyes as earth
misted with petals, some
dark red, some flesh colored—
We never thought of you
whom we were learning to worship.
We merely knew it wasn't human nature to love
only what returns love.

TRILLIUM

When I woke up I was in a forest. The dark
seemed natural, the sky through the pine trees
thick with many lights.

I knew nothing; I could do nothing but see.
And as I watched, all the lights of heaven
faded to make a single thing, a fire
burning through the cool firs.
Then it wasn't possible any longer
to stare at heaven and not be destroyed.

Are there souls that need
death's presence, as I require protection?
I think if I speak long enough
I will answer that question, I will see
whatever they see, a ladder
reaching through the firs, whatever
calls them to exchange their lives—

Think what I understand already.
I woke up ignorant in a forest;
only a moment ago, I didn't know my voice
if one were given me
would be so full of grief, my sentences
like cries strung together.
I didn't even know I felt grief
until that word came, until I felt
rain streaming from me.

LAMIUM

This is how you live when you have a cold heart.
As I do: in shadows, trailing over cool rock,
under the great maple trees.

The sun hardly touches me.
Sometimes I see it in early spring, rising very far away.
Then leaves grow over it, completely hiding it. I feel it
glinting through the leaves, erratic,
like someone hitting the side of a glass with a metal spoon.

Living things don't all require
light in the same degree. Some of us
make our own light: a silver leaf
like a path no one can use, a shallow
lake of silver in the darkness under the great maples.

But you know this already.
You and the others who think
you live for truth and, by extension, love
all that is cold.

SNOWDROPS

Do you know what I was, how I lived? You know
what despair is; then
winter should have meaning for you.

I did not expect to survive,
earth suppressing me. I didn't expect
to waken again, to feel
in damp earth my body
able to respond again, remembering
after so long how to open again
in the cold light
of earliest spring—

afraid, yes, but among you again
crying yes risk joy

in the raw wind of the new world.

CLEAR MORNING

I've watched you long enough,
I can speak to you any way I like—

I've submitted to your preferences, observing patiently
the things you love, speaking

through vehicles only, in
details of earth, as you prefer,

tendrils
of blue clematis, light

of early evening—
you would never accept

a voice like mine, indifferent
to the objects you busily name,

your mouths
small circles of awe—

And all this time
I indulged your limitation, thinking

you would cast it aside yourselves sooner or later,
thinking matter could not absorb your gaze forever—

obstacle of the clematis painting
blue flowers on the porch window—

I cannot go on
restricting myself to images

because you think it is your right
to dispute my meaning:

I am prepared now to force
clarity upon you.

SPRING SNOW

Look at the night sky:
I have two selves, two kinds of power.

I am here with you, at the window,
watching you react. Yesterday
the moon rose over moist earth in the lower garden.
Now the earth glitters like the moon,
like dead matter crusted with light.

You can close your eyes now.
I have heard your cries, and cries before yours,
and the demand behind them.
I have shown you what you want:
not belief, but capitulation
to authority, which depends on violence.

END OF WINTER

Over the still world, a bird calls
waking solitary among black boughs.

You wanted to be born; I let you be born.
When has my grief ever gotten
in the way of your pleasure?

Plunging ahead
into the dark and light at the same time
eager for sensation

as though you were some new thing, wanting
to express yourselves

all brilliance, all vivacity

never thinking
this would cost you anything,
never imagining the sound of my voice
as anything but part of you—

you won't hear it in the other world,
not clearly again,
not in birdcall or human cry,

not the clear sound, only
persistent echoing
in all sound that means good-bye, good-bye—

the one continuous line
that binds us to each other.

MATINS

Forgive me if I say I love you: the powerful
are always lied to since the weak are always
driven by panic. I cannot love
what I can't conceive, and you disclose
virtually nothing: are you like the hawthorn tree,
always the same thing in the same place,
or are you more the foxglove, inconsistent, first springing up
a pink spike on the slope behind the daisies,
and the next year, purple in the rose garden? You must see
it is useless to us, this silence that promotes belief
you must be all things, the foxglove and the hawthorn tree,
the vulnerable rose and tough daisy—we are left to think
you couldn't possibly exist. Is this
what you mean us to think, does this explain
the silence of the morning,
the crickets not yet rubbing their wings, the cats
not fighting in the yard?

MATINS

I see it is with you as with the birches:
I am not to speak to you
in the personal way. Much
has passed between us. Or
was it always only
on the one side? I am
at fault, at fault, I asked you
to be human—I am no needier
than other people. But the absence
of all feeling, of the least
concern for me—I might as well go on
addressing the birches,
as in my former life: let them
do their worst, let them
bury me with the Romantics,
their pointed yellow leaves
falling and covering me.

SCILLA

Not I, you idiot, not self, but we, we—waves
of sky blue like
a critique of heaven: why
do you treasure your voice
when to be one thing
is to be next to nothing?
Why do you look up? To hear
an echo like the voice
of god? You are all the same to us,
solitary, standing above us, planning
your silly lives: you go
where you are sent, like all things,
where the wind plants you,
one or another of you forever
looking down and seeing some image
of water, and hearing what? Waves,
and over waves, birds singing.

RETREATING WIND

When I made you, I loved you.
Now I pity you.

I gave you all you needed:
bed of earth, blanket of blue air—

As I get further away from you
I see you more clearly.
Your souls should have been immense by now,
not what they are,
small talking things—

I gave you every gift,
blue of the spring morning,
time you didn't know how to use—
you wanted more, the one gift
reserved for another creation.

Whatever you hoped,
you will not find yourselves in the garden,
among the growing plants.
Your lives are not circular like theirs:

your lives are the bird's flight
which begins and ends in stillness—
which *begins* and *ends,* in form echoing
this arc from the white birch
to the apple tree.

THE GARDEN

I couldn't do it again,
I can hardly bear to look at it—

in the garden, in light rain
the young couple planting
a row of peas, as though
no one has ever done this before,
the great difficulties have never as yet
been faced and solved—

They cannot see themselves,
in fresh dirt, starting up
without perspective,
the hills behind them pale green, clouded with flowers—

She wants to stop;
he wants to get to the end,
to stay with the thing—

Look at her, touching his cheek
to make a truce, her fingers
cool with spring rain;
in thin grass, bursts of purple crocus—

even here, even at the beginning of love,
her hand leaving his face makes
an image of departure

and they think
they are free to overlook
this sadness.

THE HAWTHORN TREE

Side by side, not
hand in hand: I watch you
walking in the summer garden—things
that can't move
learn to see; I do not need
to chase you through
the garden; human beings leave
signs of feeling
everywhere, flowers
scattered on the dirt path, all
white and gold, some
lifted a little by
the evening wind; I do not need
to follow where you are now,
deep in the poisonous field, to know
the cause of your flight, human
passion or rage: for what else
would you let drop
all you have gathered?

LOVE IN MOONLIGHT

Sometimes a man or woman forces his despair
on another person, which is called
baring the heart, alternatively, baring the soul—
meaning for this moment they acquired souls—
outside, a summer evening, a whole world
thrown away on the moon: groups of silver forms
which might be buildings or trees, the narrow garden
where the cat hides, rolling on its back in the dust,
the rose, the coreopsis, and, in the dark, the gold
    dome of the capitol
converted to an alloy of moonlight, shape
without detail, the myth, the archetype, the soul
filled with fire that is moonlight really, taken
from another source, and briefly
shining as the moon shines: stone or not,
the moon is still that much of a living thing.

APRIL

No one's despair is like my despair—

You have no place in this garden
thinking such things, producing
the tiresome outward signs; the man
pointedly weeding an entire forest,
the woman limping, refusing to change clothes
or wash her hair.

Do you suppose I care
if you speak to one another?
But I mean you to know
I expected better of two creatures
who were given minds: if not
that you would actually care for each other
at least that you would understand
grief is distributed
between you, among all your kind, for me
to know you, as deep blue
marks the wild scilla, white
the wood violet.

VIOLETS

Because in our world
something is always hidden,
small and white,
small and what you call
pure, we do not grieve
as you grieve, dear
suffering master; you
are no more lost
than we are, under
the hawthorn tree, the hawthorn holding
balanced trays of pearls: what
has brought you among us
who would teach you, though
you kneel and weep,
clasping your great hands,
in all your greatness knowing
nothing of the soul's nature,
which is never to die: poor sad god,
either you never have one
or you never lose one.

WITCHGRASS

Something
comes into the world unwelcome
calling disorder, disorder—

If you hate me so much
don't bother to give me
a name: do you need
one more slur
in your language, another
way to blame
one tribe for everything—

as we both know,
if you worship
one god, you only need
one enemy—

I'm not the enemy.
Only a ruse to ignore
what you see happening
right here in this bed,
a little paradigm
of failure. One of your precious flowers
dies here almost every day
and you can't rest until
you attack the cause, meaning

whatever is left, whatever
happens to be sturdier
than your personal passion—

It was not meant
to last forever in the real world.
But why admit that, when you can go on
doing what you always do,
mourning and laying blame,
always the two together.

I don't need your praise
to survive. I was here first,
before you were here, before
you ever planted a garden.
And I'll be here when only the sun and moon
are left, and the sea, and the wide field.

I will constitute the field.

THE JACOB'S LADDER

Trapped in the earth,
wouldn't you too want to go
to heaven? I live
in a lady's garden. Forgive me, lady;
longing has taken my grace. I am
not what you wanted. But
as men and women seem
to desire each other, I too desire
knowledge of paradise—and now
your grief, a naked stem
reaching the porch window.
And at the end, what? A small blue flower
like a star. Never
to leave the world! Is this
not what your tears mean?

MATINS

You want to know how I spend my time?
I walk the front lawn, pretending
to be weeding. You ought to know
I'm never weeding, on my knees, pulling
clumps of clover from the flower beds: in fact
I'm looking for courage, for some evidence
my life will change, though
it takes forever, checking
each clump for the symbolic
leaf, and soon the summer is ending, already
the leaves turning, always the sick trees
going first, the dying turning
brilliant yellow, while a few dark birds perform
their curfew of music. You want to see my hands?
As empty now as at the first note.
Or was the point always
to continue without a sign?

MATINS

What is my heart to you
that you must break it over and over
like a plantsman testing
his new species? Practice
on something else: how can I live
in colonies, as you prefer, if you impose
a quarantine of affliction, dividing me
from healthy members of
my own tribe: you do not do this
in the garden, segregate
the sick rose; you let it wave its sociable
infested leaves in
the faces of the other roses, and the tiny aphids
leap from plant to plant, proving yet again
I am the lowest of your creatures, following
the thriving aphid and the trailing rose— Father,
as agent of my solitude, alleviate
at least my guilt; lift
the stigma of isolation, unless
it is your plan to make me
sound forever again, as I was
sound and whole in my mistaken childhood,
or if not then, under the light weight
of my mother's heart, or if not then,
in dream, first
being that would never die.

SONG

Like a protected heart,
the blood–red
flower of the wild rose begins
to open on the lowest branch,
supported by the netted
mass of a large shrub:
it blooms against the dark
which is the heart's constant
backdrop, while flowers
higher up have wilted or rotted;
to survive
adversity merely
deepens its color. But John
objects, he thinks
if this were not a poem but
an actual garden, then
the red rose would be
required to resemble
nothing else, neither
another flower nor
the shadowy heart, at
earth level pulsing
half maroon, half crimson.

FIELD FLOWERS

What are you saying? That you want
eternal life? Are your thoughts really
as compelling as all that? Certainly
you don't look at us, don't listen to us,
on your skin
stain of sun, dust
of yellow buttercups: I'm talking
to you, you staring through
bars of high grass shaking
your little rattle— O
the soul! the soul! Is it enough
only to look inward? Contempt
for humanity is one thing, but why
disdain the expansive
field, your gaze rising over the clear heads
of the wild buttercups into what? Your poor
idea of heaven: absence
of change. Better than earth? How
would you know, who are neither
here nor there, standing in our midst?

THE RED POPPY

The great thing
is not having
a mind. Feelings:
oh, I have those; they
govern me. I have
a lord in heaven
called the sun, and open
for him, showing him
the fire of my own heart, fire
like his presence.
What could such glory be
if not a heart? Oh my brothers and sisters,
were you like me once, long ago,
before you were human? Did you
permit yourselves
to open once, who would never
open again? Because in truth
I am speaking now
the way you do. I speak
because I am shattered.

CLOVER

What is dispersed
among us, which you call
the sign of blessedness
although it is, like us,
a weed, a thing
to be rooted out—

by what logic
do you hoard
a single tendril
of something you want
dead?

If there is any presence among us
so powerful, should it not
multiply, in service
of the adored garden?

You should be asking
these questions yourself,
not leaving them
to your victims. You should know
that when you swagger among us
I hear two voices speaking,
one your spirit, one
the acts of your hands.

MATINS

Not the sun merely but the earth
itself shines, white fire
leaping from the showy mountains
and the flat road
shimmering in early morning: is this
for us only, to induce
response, or are you
stirred also, helpless
to control yourself
in earth's presence—I am ashamed
at what I thought you were,
distant from us, regarding us
as an experiment: it is
a bitter thing to be
the disposable animal,
a bitter thing. Dear friend,
dear trembling partner, what
surprises you most in what you feel,
earth's radiance or your own delight?
For me, always
the delight is the surprise.

HEAVEN AND EARTH

Where one finishes, the other begins.
On top, a band of blue; underneath,
a band of green and gold, green and deep rose.

John stands at the horizon: he wants
both at once, he wants
everything at once.

The extremes are easy. Only
the middle is a puzzle. Midsummer—
everything is possible.

Meaning: never again will life end.

How can I leave my husband
standing in the garden
dreaming this sort of thing, holding
his rake, triumphantly
preparing to announce this discovery

as the fire of the summer sun
truly does stall
being entirely contained by
the burning maples
at the garden's border.

THE DOORWAY

I wanted to stay as I was
still as the world is never still,
not in midsummer but the moment before
the first flower forms, the moment
nothing is as yet past—

not midsummer, the intoxicant,
but late spring, the grass not yet
high at the edge of the garden, the early tulips
beginning to open—

like a child hovering in a doorway, watching the others,
the ones who go first,
a tense cluster of limbs, alert to
the failures of others, the public falterings

with a child's fierce confidence of imminent power
preparing to defeat
these weaknesses, to succumb
to nothing, the time directly

prior to flowering, the epoch of mastery

before the appearance of the gift,
before possession.

MIDSUMMER

How can I help you when you all want
different things—sunlight and shadow,
moist darkness, dry heat—

Listen to yourselves, vying with one another—

And you wonder
why I despair of you,
you think something could fuse you into a whole—

the still air of high summer
tangled with a thousand voices

each calling out
some need, some absolute

and in that name continually
strangling each other
in the open field—

For what? For space and air?
The privilege of being
single in the eyes of heaven?

You were not intended
to be unique. You were
my embodiment, all diversity

not what you think you see
searching the bright sky over the field,
your incidental souls
fixed like telescopes on some
enlargement of yourselves—

Why would I make you if I meant
to limit myself
to the ascendant sign,
the star, the fire, the fury?

VESPERS

Once I believed in you; I planted a fig tree.
Here, in Vermont, country
of no summer. It was a test: if the tree lived,
it would mean you existed.

By this logic, you do not exist. Or you exist
exclusively in warmer climates,
in fervent Sicily and Mexico and California,
where are grown the unimaginable
apricot and fragile peach. Perhaps
they see your face in Sicily; here, we barely see
the hem of your garment. I have to discipline myself
to share with John and Noah the tomato crop.

If there is justice in some other world, those
like myself, whom nature forces
into lives of abstinence, should get
the lion's share of all things, all
objects of hunger, greed being
praise of you. And no one praises
more intensely than I, with more
painfully checked desire, or more deserves
to sit at your right hand, if it exists, partaking
of the perishable, the immortal fig,
which does not travel.

VESPERS

In your extended absence, you permit me
use of earth, anticipating
some return on investment. I must report
failure in my assignment, principally
regarding the tomato plants.
I think I should not be encouraged to grow
tomatoes. Or, if I am, you should withhold
the heavy rains, the cold nights that come
so often here, while other regions get
twelve weeks of summer. All this
belongs to you: on the other hand,
I planted the seeds, I watched the first shoots
like wings tearing the soil, and it was my heart
broken by the blight, the black spot so quickly
multiplying in the rows. I doubt
you have a heart, in our understanding of
that term. You who do not discriminate
between the dead and the living, who are, in consequence,
immune to foreshadowing, you may not know
how much terror we bear, the spotted leaf,
the red leaves of the maple falling
even in August, in early darkness: I am responsible
for these vines.

VESPERS

More than you love me, very possibly
you love the beasts of the field, even,
possibly, the field itself, in August dotted
with wild chicory and aster:
I know. I have compared myself
to those flowers, their range of feeling
so much smaller and without issue; also to white sheep,
actually gray: I am uniquely
suited to praise you. Then why
torment me? I study the hawkweed,
the buttercup protected from the grazing herd
by being poisonous: is pain
your gift to make me
conscious in my need of you, as though
I must need you to worship you,
or have you abandoned me
in favor of the field, the stoic lambs turning
silver in twilight; waves of wild aster and chicory shining
pale blue and deep blue, since you already know
how like your raiment it is.

DAISIES

Go ahead: say what you're thinking. The garden
is not the real world. Machines
are the real world. Say frankly what any fool
could read in your face: it makes sense
to avoid us, to resist
nostalgia. It is
not modern enough, the sound the wind makes
stirring a meadow of daisies: the mind
cannot shine following it. And the mind
wants to shine, plainly, as
machines shine, and not
grow deep, as, for example, roots. It is very touching,
all the same, to see you cautiously
approaching the meadow's border in early morning,
when no one could possibly
be watching you. The longer you stand at the edge,
the more nervous you seem. No one wants to hear
impressions of the natural world: you will be
laughed at again; scorn will be piled on you.
As for what you're actually
hearing this morning: think twice
before you tell anyone what was said in this field
and by whom.

END OF SUMMER

After all things occurred to me,
the void occurred to me.

There is a limit
to the pleasure I had in form—

I am not like you in this,
I have no release in another body,

I have no need
of shelter outside myself—

My poor inspired
creation, you are
distractions, finally,
mere curtailment; you are
too little like me in the end
to please me.

And so adamant—
you want to be paid off
for your disappearance,
all paid in some part of the earth,
some souvenir, as you were once
rewarded for labor,
the scribe being paid
in silver, the shepherd in barley

although it is not earth
that is lasting, not
these small chips of matter—

If you would open your eyes
you would see me, you would see
the emptiness of heaven
mirrored on earth, the fields
vacant again, lifeless, covered with snow—

then white light
no longer disguised as matter.

VESPERS

I don't wonder where you are anymore.
You're in the garden; you're where John is,
in the dirt, abstracted, holding his green trowel.
This is how he gardens: fifteen minutes of intense effort,
fifteen minutes of ecstatic contemplation. Sometimes
I work beside him, doing the shade chores,
weeding, thinning the lettuces; sometimes I watch
from the porch near the upper garden until twilight makes
lamps of the first lilies: all this time,
peace never leaves him. But it rushes through me,
not as sustenance the flower holds
but like bright light through the bare tree.

VESPERS

Even as you appeared to Moses, because
I need you, you appear to me, not
often, however. I live essentially
in darkness. You are perhaps training me to be
responsive to the slightest brightening. Or, like the poets,
are you stimulated by despair, does grief
move you to reveal your nature? This afternoon,
in the physical world to which you commonly
contribute your silence, I climbed
the small hill above the wild blueberries, metaphysically
descending, as on all my walks: did I go deep enough
for you to pity me, as you have sometimes pitied
others who suffer, favoring those
with theological gifts? As you anticipated,
I did not look up. So you came down to me:
at my feet, not the wax
leaves of the wild blueberry but your fiery self, a whole
pasture of fire, and beyond, the red sun neither falling
        nor rising—
I was not a child; I could take advantage of illusions.

VESPERS

You thought we didn't know. But we knew once,
children know these things. Don't turn away now—
    we inhabited
a lie to appease you. I remember
sunlight of early spring, embankments
netted with dark vinca. I remember
lying in a field, touching my brother's body.
Don't turn away now; we denied
memory to console you. We mimicked you, reciting
the terms of our punishment. I remember
some of it, not all of it: deceit
begins as forgetting. I remember small things, flowers
growing under the hawthorn tree, bells
of the wild scilla. Not all, but enough
to know you exist: who else had reason to create
mistrust between a brother and sister but the one
who profited, to whom we turned in solitude? Who else
would so envy the bond we had then
as to tell us it was not earth
but heaven we were losing?

EARLY DARKNESS

How can you say
earth should give me joy? Each thing
born is my burden; I cannot succeed
with all of you.

And you would like to dictate to me,
you would like to tell me
who among you is most valuable,
who most resembles me.
And you hold up as an example
the pure life, the detachment
you struggle to achieve—

How can you understand me
when you cannot understand yourselves?
Your memory is not
powerful enough, it will not
reach back far enough—

Never forget you are my children.
You are not suffering because you touched each other
but because you were born,
because you required life
separate from me.

HARVEST

It grieves me to think of you in the past—

Look at you, blindly clinging to earth
as though it were the vineyards of heaven
while the fields go up in flames around you—

Ah, little ones, how unsubtle you are:
it is at once the gift and the torment.

If what you fear in death
is punishment beyond this, you need not
fear death:

how many times must I destroy my own creation
to teach you
this is your punishment:

with one gesture I established you
in time and in paradise.

THE WHITE ROSE

This is the earth? Then
I don't belong here.

Who are you in the lighted window,
shadowed now by the flickering leaves
of the wayfarer tree?
Can you survive where I won't last
beyond the first summer?

All night the slender branches of the tree
shift and rustle at the bright window.
Explain my life to me, you who make no sign,

though I call out to you in the night:
I am not like you, I have only
my body for a voice; I can't
disappear into silence—

And in the cold morning
over the dark surface of the earth
echoes of my voice drift,
whiteness steadily absorbed into darkness

as though you were making a sign after all
to convince me you too couldn't survive here

or to show me you are not the light I called to
but the blackness behind it.

IPOMOEA

What was my crime in another life,
as in this life my crime
is sorrow, that I am not to be
permitted to ascend ever again,
never in any sense
permitted to repeat my life,
wound in the hawthorn, all
earthly beauty my punishment
as it is yours—
Source of my suffering, why
have you drawn from me
these flowers like the sky, except
to mark me as a part
of my master: I am
his cloak's color, my flesh giveth
form to his glory.

PRESQUE ISLE

In every life, there's a moment or two.
In every life, a room somewhere, by the sea or
    in the mountains.

On the table, a dish of apricots. Pits in a white ashtray.

Like all images, these were the conditions of a pact:
on your cheek, tremor of sunlight,
my finger pressing your lips.
The walls blue-white; paint from the low bureau
    flaking a little.

That room must still exist, on the fourth floor,
with a small balcony overlooking the ocean.
A square white room, the top sheet pulled back over
    the edge of the bed.
It hasn't dissolved back into nothing, into reality.
Through the open window, sea air, smelling of iodine.

Early morning: a man calling a small boy back from the water.
That small boy—he would be twenty now.

Around your face, rushes of damp hair, streaked with
    auburn.
Muslin, flicker of silver. Heavy jar filled with white peonies.

RETREATING LIGHT

You were like very young children,
always waiting for a story.
And I'd been through it all too many times;
I was tired of telling stories.
So I gave you the pencil and paper.
I gave you pens made of reeds
I had gathered myself, afternoons in the dense meadows.
I told you, write your own story.

After all those years of listening
I thought you'd know
what a story was.

All you could do was weep.
You wanted everything told to you
and nothing thought through yourselves.

Then I realized you couldn't think
with any real boldness or passion;
you hadn't had your own lives yet,
your own tragedies.
So I gave you lives, I gave you tragedies,
because apparently tools alone weren't enough.

You will never know how deeply
it pleases me to see you sitting there
like independent beings,
to see you dreaming by the open window,

holding the pencils I gave you
until the summer morning disappears into writing.

Creation has brought you
great excitement, as I knew it would,
as it does in the beginning.
And I am free to do as I please now,
to attend to other things, in confidence
you have no need of me anymore.

VESPERS

I know what you planned, what you meant to do, teaching me
to love the world, making it impossible
to turn away completely, to shut it out completely
        ever again—
it is everywhere; when I close my eyes,
birdsong, scent of lilac in early spring, scent of summer roses:
you mean to take it away, each flower, each connection
        with earth—
why would you wound me, why would you want me
desolate in the end, unless you wanted me so starved for hope
I would refuse to see that finally
nothing was left to me, and would believe instead
in the end you were left to me.

VESPERS: PAROUSIA

Love of my life, you
are lost and I am
young again.

A few years pass.
The air fills
with girlish music;
in the front yard
the apple tree is
studded with blossoms.

I try to win you back,
that is the point
of the writing.
But you are gone forever,
as in Russian novels, saying
a few words I don't remember—

How lush the world is,
how full of things that don't belong to me—

I watch the blossoms shatter,
no longer pink,
but old, old, a yellowish white—
the petals seem
to float on the bright grass,
fluttering slightly.

What a nothing you were,

to be changed so quickly
into an image, an odor—
you are everywhere, source
of wisdom and anguish.

VESPERS

Your voice is gone now; I hardly hear you.
Your starry voice all shadow now
and the earth dark again
with your great changes of heart.

And by day the grass going brown in places
under the broad shadows of the maple trees.
Now, everywhere I am talked to by silence

so it is clear I have no access to you;
I do not exist for you, you have drawn
a line through my name.

In what contempt do you hold us
to believe only loss can impress
your power on us,

the first rains of autumn shaking the white lilies—

When you go, you go absolutely,
deducting visible life from all things

but not all life,
lest we turn from you.

VESPERS

End of August. Heat
like a tent over
John's garden. And some things
have the nerve to be getting started,
clusters of tomatoes, stands
of late lilies—optimism
of the great stalks—imperial
gold and silver: but why
start anything
so close to the end?
Tomatoes that will never ripen, lilies
winter will kill, that won't
come back in spring. Or
are you thinking
I spend too much time
looking ahead, like
an old woman wearing
sweaters in summer;
are you saying I can
flourish, having
no hope
of enduring? Blaze of the red cheek, glory
of the open throat, white,
spotted with crimson.

SUNSET

My great happiness
is the sound your voice makes
calling to me even in despair; my sorrow
that I cannot answer you
in speech you accept as mine.

You have no faith in your own language.
So you invest
authority in signs
you cannot read with any accuracy.

And yet your voice reaches me always.
And I answer constantly,
my anger passing
as winter passes. My tenderness
should be apparent to you
in the breeze of the summer evening
and in the words that become
your own response.

LULLABY

Time to rest now; you have had
enough excitement for the time being.

Twilight, then early evening. Fireflies
in the room, flickering here and there, here and there,
and summer's deep sweetness filling the open window.

Don't think of these things anymore.
Listen to my breathing, your own breathing
like the fireflies, each small breath
a flare in which the world appears.

I've sung to you long enough in the summer night.
I'll win you over in the end; the world can't give you
this sustained vision.

You must be taught to love me. Human beings must be
    taught to love
silence and darkness.

THE SILVER LILY

The nights have grown cool again, like the nights
of early spring, and quiet again. Will
speech disturb you? We're
alone now; we have no reason for silence.

Can you see, over the garden—the full moon rises.
I won't see the next full moon.

In spring, when the moon rose, it meant
time was endless. Snowdrops
opened and closed, the clustered
seeds of the maples fell in pale drifts.
White over white, the moon rose over the birch tree.
And in the crook, where the tree divides,
leaves of the first daffodils, in moonlight
soft greenish-silver.

We have come too far together toward the end now
to fear the end. These nights, I am no longer even certain
I know what the end means. And you, who've been
                with a man—

after the first cries,
doesn't joy, like fear, make no sound?

SEPTEMBER TWILIGHT

I gathered you together,
I can dispense with you—

I'm tired of you, chaos
of the living world—
I can only extend myself
for so long to a living thing.

I summoned you into existence
by opening my mouth, by lifting
my little finger, shimmering

blues of the wild
aster, blossom
of the lily, immense,
gold-veined—

you come and go; eventually
I forget your names.

You come and go, every one of you
flawed in some way,
in some way compromised: you are worth
one life, no more than that.

I gathered you together;
I can erase you
as though you were a draft to be thrown away,

an exercise

because I've finished you, vision
of deepest mourning.

THE GOLD LILY

As I perceive
I am dying now and know
I will not speak again, will not
survive the earth, be summoned
out of it again, not
a flower yet, a spine only, raw dirt
catching my ribs, I call you,
father and master: all around,
my companions are failing, thinking
you do not see. How
can they know you see
unless you save us?
In the summer twilight, are you
close enough to hear
your child's terror? Or
are you not my father,
you who raised me?

THE WHITE LILIES

As a man and woman make
a garden between them like
a bed of stars, here
they linger in the summer evening
and the evening turns
cold with their terror: it
could all end, it is capable
of devastation. All, all
can be lost, through scented air
the narrow columns
uselessly rising, and beyond,
a churning sea of poppies—

Hush, beloved. It doesn't matter to me
how many summers I live to return:
this one summer we have entered eternity.
I felt your two hands
bury me to release its splendor.

ABOUT THE AUTHOR

Louise Glück is the author of nine books of poems and a collection of essays, *Proofs and Theories*, which won the PEN/Martha Albrand Award. She was awarded the National Book Critics Circle Award for *The Triumph of Achilles*, the Pulitzer Prize for *The Wild Iris*, and the first annual *New Yorker* Readers Award and the Bollingen Prize for *Vita Nova*. Among her many other awards are the Bobbitt National Prize for Poetry from the Library of Congress, the William Carlos Williams award from the Poetry Society of America, a Lannan Foundation Award, and the Ambassador's Award from the English Speaking Union. Louise Glück is a Fellow of the American Academy of Arts and Letters and teaches at Williams College. She lives in Cambridge, Massachusetts.